tiger tales

5 River Road, Suite 128, Wilton, CT 06897
Published in the United States 2018
Originally published in Great Britain 2018
by Little Tiger Press
Text and illustrations copyright © 2018 Jonny Lambert
ISBN-13: 978-1-68010-081-5
ISBN-10: 1-68010-081-5
Printed in China
LTP/ 1400/1979/0817

For more insight and activities, visit us at www.tigertalesbooks.com

LOOK OUT!
It's a Dragon!

by Jonny Lambert

tiger tales

Sapphire wasn't like other dragons.
She didn't want to crush castles
or capture princesses.

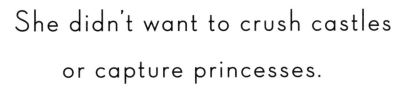

And sitting on cold, rocky
mountains just hurt her bottom.
"That's it," said Sapphire. "I'm off!"
She searched far and wide until she found . . .

. . . a sunny place filled with trees.

"Hello, neighbors!" beamed Sapphire, landing

WHOOSH! in a field full of flowers.

"Look out! It's a dragon!" cried the animals.

"Run!"

"Don't run away!
It's so nice here,"
Sapphire sighed happily,
wriggling in the
long, soft grass.

But from behind her, a little voice squeaked,

"Hey!
You're squashing me!
You can't stay here!"

"But I love it!" replied Sapphire. "Why can't I stay?"

"Because you're a **dragon!**" Mouse exclaimed.
"We know what dragons do. They chase us
with their fiery flames."

"**Not me**," said Sapphire.
"I'm a friendly dragon. **Look!**"

And she picked a snack
for Mouse.

"Thank you," squeaked Mouse,
a little surprised.

But just then, Sapphire's nose began to itch . . .

"AAAACHOOOO!"

Sapphire sneezed an **enormous** sneeze and
accidentally singed Warbler's tail.

"Eek!"

squeaked Mouse.

"Argh!"

cried Warbler.

"I've been scorched by
a **dragon!**

And now
it's coming
after me!"

Sapphire **swooped**

after the songbird.

"Please come back. You've got it wrong—
I just want to be your friend!"

But Warbler didn't stop,
so Sapphire followed her . . .

CRASH!
SMASH!
SPLINTER!

. . . toppling birds from their treetops.

"Ahhh!"

cried the animals.
"A dragon is wrecking our homes!"

Enough was enough.

"STOP, you lumbering beast!"
bellowed Mouse. "You can't live here.
Leave us alone!"

Sapphire's ears drooped, and she shuffled away.
"It really was a perfect home,"
she sniffed sadly.

"Good riddance!" muttered Mouse,
and the animals settled down for a nap.

But as they slept,

eerie shadows crept.

Closer and **larger**, the shadows loomed. Then . . .

The animals scattered this way and that,
chased by **fiery, scary dragons!**

"Help!" they cried.
"Somebody help us!"

And somebody did!

Whoosh!

"Nobody hurts my friends!" cried Sapphire, swooping in and chasing off the dragons.

"Thank you, Sapphire!" the animals cheered. "We're sorry we told you to leave."

But their home was scorched
"We can't stay here,"
said Mouse.

So Sapphire took off and searched far and wide
until she found . . .

. . . a happy new home for all of them!

"It's perfect!" cried the animals.

And it was.

There was sunshine and flowers, and space for everyone, even the biggest of friends.